DATE DUE			

E
BRO

Brown, Ruth

Alphabet times
four

BTSB Bound to Stay Bound Books, Inc.

CUNNINGHAM

Alphabet Times Four

AN INTERNATIONAL ABC

ENGLISH   SPANISH   FRENCH   GERMAN

Ruth Brown

DUTTON CHILDREN'S BOOKS · NEW YORK

CUNNINGHAM

copyright © 1991 by Ruth Brown

All rights reserved.

CIP Data is available.

First published in the United States 1991 by
Dutton Children's Books,
a division of Penguin Books USA Inc.

Originally published in Great Britain by Andersen Press Ltd., 20 Vauxhill Bridge Road, London SW1V 2SA.
Published in Australia by Century Hutchinson Pty. Ltd., 89-91 Albion Street, Surry Hills, NSW 2010.
Color separated by Photolitho AG Offsetreproduktionen, Gossau, Zurich, Switzerland.
Printed in Italy by Grafiche AZ, Verona.

First American Edition

ISBN 0-525-44831-4   10 9 8 7 6 5 4 3 2 1

A   a

ark   **arca**   **arche**   **Arche**
ark   AR-kah   arsh   AR-kheh

B b

ball   **bola**   **boule**   **Ball**

bawl   BOH-la   bool   bahl

C

c

chameleon
kah-MEEL-yon

camaleón
kah-mah-leh-ON

caméléon
kah-may-lay-ONH

Chamäleon
kah-MEH-leh-on

D   d

dragon   **dragón**   **dragon**   **Drache**

DRAG-en   drah-GON   drah-GONH   DRAH-kheh

E
e

elephant
EL-e-fant

elefante
eh-leh-FAHN-teh

éléphant
ay-lay-FONH

Elefant
eh-leh-FAHNT

F f

fire   **fuego**   **feu**   **Feuer**

FY-er   FWEH-go   fuh   FOY-er

G

g

gorilla
gah-RIL-ah

gorila
go-REE-lah

gorille
gah-REE-yuh

Gorilla
go-RI-lah

H h

hamster   **hamster**   **hamster**   **Hamster**

HAM-ster   AM-stehr   ahm-STAIR   HAHM-stehr

I i

insect   insecto   insecte   Insekt
IN-sekt   een-SEK-toh   anh-SEKT   in-SEKT

J

j

jaguar
JAG-wahr

jaguar
hah-GWAHR

jaguar
zhah-GWAHR

Jaguar
ya-gu-WAHR

K

k

kiwi	kiwi	kiwi	Kiwi
KEE-wee	KEE-wee	kee-WEE	KEE-vee

L l

labyrinth	**laberinto**	**labyrinthe**	**Labyrinth**
LAB-i-rinth	lah-beh-REEN-toh	lah-beer-ANHT	lah-bur-RINT

M

m

magic
MAJ-ik

magia
MAKH-ya

magie
mah-ZHEE

Magie
ma-GHEE

N

n

nose   **nariz**   **nez**   **Nase**

noze   nah-REESS   nay   NAH-zeh

O o

orchid	orquídea	orchidée	Orchidee
OR-kid	or-KEE-theh-ah	or-kee-DAY	or-khee-DAY-yeh

P

P

pyramid
PEER-a-mid

pirámide
pee-RAH-mee-theh

pyramide
peer-ah-MEED

Pyramide
pur-ah-MEE-deh

quintet
kwin-TET

quinteto
keen-TEH-toh

quintette
kanh-TETT

Quintett
kvin-TET

R r

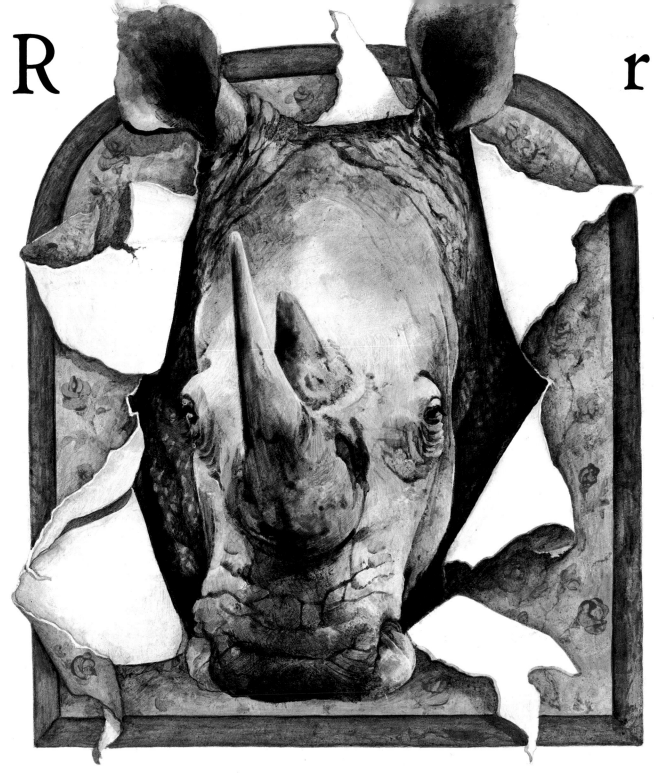

rhinoceros
ry-NAH-ser-us

rinoceronte
ree-no-seh-RON-teh

rhinocéros
ree-no-sayr-OSS

Rhinozeros
ree-NO-tsehr-os

S   s

snake **serpiente** **serpent** **Schlange**
snayk   sehr-PYEN-teh   sair-PONH   SHLAHNG-eh

T

t

tiger
TY-gur

tigre
TEE-greh

tigre
teegr

Tiger
TEE-gehr

U   u

universe
YOO-nuh-vurs

universo
oo-nee-VEHR-so

univers
oon-nee-VAIR

Universum
oo-nee-VEHR-zoom

CUNNINGHAM

V v

volcano volcán volcan Vulkan

vol-CAY-no bol-KAHN vul-KANH vool-KAHN

W   **W**

water polo	water-polo*	water-polo	Wasserball
WAH-tur po-lo	WAH-tehr-po-lo	vah-tair-po-LO	VAH-sehr-bahl

also polo-acuático

X   X

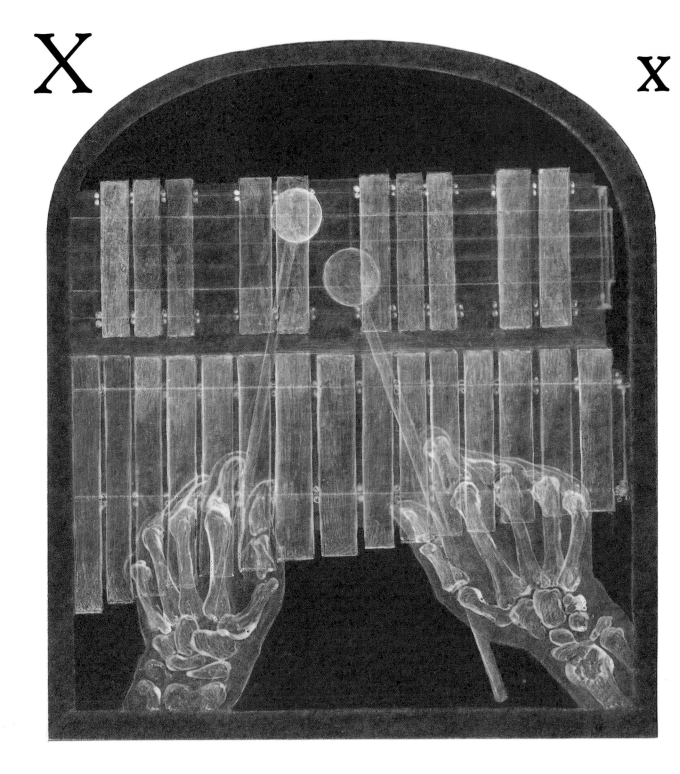

xylophone   **xilófono**   **xylophone**   **Xylophon**
ZY-luh-fone   ksee-LOH-foh-noh   ksee-loh-FUN   ksu-loh-FONE

Y   y

yeti   yeti   yeti   Yeti
YET-ee   YEH-tee   yeh-TEE   YET-ee

Z z

zigzag
ZIG-zag

zigzag
tseeg-TSAHG

zig-zag
zeeg-ZAHG

Zickzack
TSIK-tsak

		English	Spanish	French	German
A	a	ark	arca	arche	Arche
B	b	ball	bola	boule	Ball
C	c	chameleon	camaleón	caméléon	Chamäleon
D	d	dragon	dragón	dragon	Drache
E	e	elephant	elefante	éléphant	Elefant
F	f	fire	fuego	feu	Feuer
G	g	gorilla	gorila	gorille	Gorilla
H	h	hamster	hamster	hamster	Hamster
I	i	insect	insecto	insecte	Insekt
J	j	jaguar	jaguar	jaguar	Jaguar
K	k	kiwi	kiwi	kiwi	Kiwi
L	l	labyrinth	laberinto	labyrinthe	Labyrinth
M	m	magic	magia	magie	Magie
N	n	nose	nariz	nez	Nase
O	o	orchid	orquídea	orchidée	Orchidee
P	p	pyramid	pirámide	pyramide	Pyramide
Q	q	quintet	quinteto	quintette	Quintett
R	r	rhinoceros	rinoceronte	rhinocéros	Rhinozeros
S	s	snake	serpiente	serpent	Schlange
T	t	tiger	tigre	tigre	Tiger
U	u	universe	universo	univers	Universum
V	v	volcano	volcán	volcan	Vulkan
W	w	water polo	water-polo	water-polo	Wasserball
X	x	xylophone	xilófono	xylophone	Xylophon
Y	y	yeti	yeti	yeti	Yeti
Z	z	zigzag	zigzag	zig-zag	Zickzack

Notes

As you may have noticed, words in different languages may share the same roots. For example, *volcano, volcán, volcan,* and *Vulkan* all come from the Latin *vulcan.* Languages often borrow whole words from each other, too. *Yeti* first came from the Tibetan language, and *kiwi* is a Maori word from New Guinea.

Two additional letters of the Spanish alphabet have not been illustrated in this book. They are *ll,* as in *llave* (key), and *ñ,* as in *piña* (pineapple).

In the French pronunciation key, -NH is a nasal sound that English does not have. To practice this sound, pinch your nose shut and say these words aloud: *in, an, on.*

All nouns are capitalized in German.